BORN IN THE GRAVY

DENYS CAZET

ORCHARD BOOKS   NEW YORK

Orchard Books, 95 Madison Avenue, New York, NY 10016

Manufactured in the United States of America. Printed by Barton Press, Inc.
Bound by Horowitz/Rae. Book design by Mina Greenstein.
The text of this book is set in 16 point Gamma Book. The illustrations are colored
pencil reproduced in full color.   10   9   8   7   6   5   4   3   2   1

93B6434

Library of Congress Cataloging-in-Publication Data
Cazet, Denys. Born in the gravy / Denys Cazet.   p.   cm.
"A Richard Jackson book."
Summary: A young Mexican American girl tells her father all the things she did on
her first day in kindergarten.
ISBN 0-531-05488-8.   ISBN 0-531-08638-0 (lib. bdg.)
[1. Kindergarten—Fiction. 2. Schools—Fiction. 3. Fathers and daughters—Fiction.
4. Mexican Americans—Fiction.]   I. Title. PZ7.C2985Bo   1993   [E]—dc20   92-44523

 For my grandson Casey

"*¡Papá!*" Margarita shouted. "I'm a kindergartner!"

Margarita's father smiled and gave her a big hug. "*Vamos*," he said. "Let's go get an ice cream cone."

Margarita sat down at a little table. She saw some other kindergartners and waved.

"Two scoops of chocolate chip," said Papá. "*¡El preferido de Margarita!*"

"My favorite!" said Margarita, waving to another little girl.

"*¡Amigos nuevos!*" said Papá.

Margarita licked her ice cream cone. "That's Susie. She cried most of the day."

Papá poured milk into his coffee. "She missed her mother."

"This morning *Mamá* cried," said Margarita.
"She used up all her handkerchiefs."

My best tie, my best suit, and my name is upside-down and backwards!

"*¿Y Margarita? ¿Triste también?*" asked Papá, stirring his coffee.

"*Sí*, a little sad," said Margarita. "But happy, too! The teacher is nice. She showed us our cubbies. Mine has my name on it. It's where I put my lunch. Unless I have a hot lunch. Then I need a red chip. A white chip is for milk. You put your name in the wall pocket. You hang your name tag around your neck. Then you sit in the circle."

"So many jobs," said Papá.

"School *IS* my job," said Margarita.

"This circle . . . what do you do there?"

"Wait," said Margarita. "Some kids went to the wrong room. The teacher's helper had to bring them back."

Papá leaned over and whispered, "Susie . . . she stopped crying?"

"Sort of," Margarita said softly, "but she started again when the box on the wall shouted, *'WELCOME TO KINDERGARTEN!'*"

"What did the *maestra* do?"

"She played the piano. We sang 'Good Morning to You.' Susie can cry and sing at the same time."

WELCOME TO KINDERGARTEN

I pledge allegiance to the flag of the United States of America, and to the Republicans for which it . . .

"Everybody has a job," Margarita continued. "Max leads the pledge. Lupe and Peter help clean up. Jolene and I take the teacher's notes to the office."

Papá sipped his coffee. *"Mucho trabajo."*

"A lot of work!" said Margarita. "It's a long trip, too. We saw lots of big kids. There are no little kids in our school."

"¿Ni siquiera uno?"

"Not one!" said Margarita.

"And when you came back?"

"We drew a dead bug. It had six legs, some wings, and a body like a hot dog."

Margarita gave Papá a taste of her ice cream.

"Was I born in the gravy?" she asked.

"*¿Nacida en la salsa?*" said Papá. "Where did you hear that?"

"Recess," said Margarita. "Some first graders said we were kindergarten babies, born in the gravy. Was I?"

"No," said Papá. "You were born in Guadalajara!"

"Ohh!" said Margarita.

Papá smiled. "*¿Después de* recess?"

"We sat in the circle and waited."

"*¿Por qué?* Why?" asked Papá.

"Too many kids," said Margarita. "After the teacher's helper took them back to their room, we worked on our colors. This is red week. Tomorrow I'm going to wear my red dress."

"You will be *preciosa!*" declared Papá.

Margarita fluffed her hair. "Can you guess what we had for lunch?"

Papá shook his head.

"Wonder beans."

"What was in the *frijoles?*"

"Allergies," said Margarita. "Juan Alberto's face swelled up. The nurse said there were allergies in the beans."

"*¡Pobrecito!*" said Papá.

"Juan felt better after the fire engines came," said Margarita. "*¿Un fuego?*"

"No, *Papá.* There was no fire. Archie climbed up a tree and wouldn't come down. He told the principal he wasn't going to talk to strangers."

"The fire trucks got him down?"

"No," said Margarita. "Archie came down by himself. They called the fire department to get the principal down."

Papá laughed. *"Bien entendido."*

"Fire engines are red," said Margarita. "It's red week, *Papá.*"

Margarita leaned on the table. "After lunch we rested."

Papá refilled his coffee cup. *"Bueno, bueno,"* he said.

"Then we had math, a story, and drew a picture of our day."

"What did you learn?"

"We counted red beans," said Margarita. "Fernando stuck two beans up his nose. When the teacher's helper tried to get them out, Fernando blew them across the room."

"How far?" Papá asked.

Margarita shrugged. "Two beans, take away two beans, is no beans," said Margarita.

Papá nodded. "What was the story?"

"'Little Red Riding Hood.' And for my picture, I drew everyone in our family that I missed today. I had to turn the paper sideways."

"There are many proud parents today," said Papá, "but I am the proudest."

Margarita fluffed her hair again.

"Do you want to hear the 'Good-bye Song'?" Margarita asked.

"*Por favor,*" said Papá.

Margarita walked over to Susie and whispered in her ear. Susie smiled and took Margarita's hand.

They sang,

> "Good-bye, *adiós,* our day is done,
> Today we learned we're number one.
> We are kindergartners, we're the best,
> We work all day with little rest.
> Tomorrow we'll do it all again,
> So, *hasta mañana*—see you then!"

When they finished, they bowed and sat down together.

"*¡Magnífico!*" said Papá.